Penny
AND HER SONG

KEVIN HENKES

SCHOLASTIC INC.

No part of this publication may be reproduced, stored in a retrieval
system, or transmitted in any form or by any means, electronic,
mechanical, photocopying, recording, or otherwise, without written
permission of the publisher. For information regarding permission,
write to Greenwillow Books, an imprint of HarperCollins Publishers,
10 East 53rd Street, New York, NY 10022.

ISBN 978-0-545-49799-2

12   16 17/0

Printed in the U.S.A.   40

First Scholastic printing, September 2012

Watercolor paints and a black pen were used to prepare the full-color art.
The text type is Century Schoolbook.

For Penryth

Chapter 1

Penny came home from school
with a song.

"Listen, Mama," said Penny.

"It's my very own song."

Penny started to sing,

"One is nice—"

"Your song is beautiful," said Mama,

"but you will wake up the babies."

So Penny looked for Papa.

"Listen, Papa," said Penny.

"It's my very own song."

　Penny started to sing,

"One is nice, two is nice—"

"Your song is wonderful," said Papa,

"but the babies are asleep."

So Penny went to her room
and shut the door.
Penny started to sing,
"One is nice, two is nice,
three is even better . . ."

Penny stopped.

She wanted someone

to listen to her.

Penny sang to herself

in the mirror.

That didn't work.

Penny sang

to her glass animals.

That didn't work, either.

Penny made faces at herself
in the mirror.

Then she moved her glass animals
around on the top
of her dresser.

She almost forgot about her song.

Chapter 2

Soon it was time to eat.

"Listen, everyone," said Penny.

"It's my very own song."

Penny started to sing,

"One is nice, two is nice,

three is even better.

Four is nice—"

"Not at

the table,"

said Mama.

"After dinner,"

said Papa.

After dinner Penny sang

for Mama and Papa

and the babies.

This was Penny's song:

"One is nice, two is nice,

Three is even better.

Four is nice, five is nice,

Six in rain is wetter.

Seven is nice, eight is nice,

Nine is almost best.

But ten is even bigger,

And is better than the rest."

"That was beautiful!" said Mama.

"That was wonderful!" said Papa.

The babies made baby noises.

"Thank you," said Penny.

Penny sang her song again.

Then everyone sang Penny's song.

Mama sang high and softly.

Papa sang low and loudly.

Penny sang in the middle

and clearly.

Beautifully.

The babies sang

in their own baby way.

Then they did a little show.

Mama wore funny sunglasses.

Papa wore a silly hat.

Penny wore her feather boa.

The babies wore

what they were wearing.

They all sang and sang

and sang.

"I'm tired," said Mama.

She flopped onto a chair.

"I'm tired," said Papa.

He plopped onto the sofa.

The babies were tired.

They fell asleep

in their basket.

Mama laughed.

"At first I thought you would

wake up the babies," she said.

"And now," said Papa,

"you have helped them

fall asleep."

Penny yawned.

She was tired, too.

"We had a good time,"

said Penny.

"Speaking of time," said Mama.

"Do you know what time it is now?"

"Time to sing it again?"

said Penny.

"No," said Papa. "Time for bed."

Mama turned off
the light.

Papa picked up
the babies.

Penny led
the way upstairs.

Everyone kissed everyone.

"Will I remember my song
  in the morning?" asked Penny.

"Yes," said Mama.

"Are you sure?" asked Penny.

"Yes," said Papa.

And they were right.

Penny remembered her song.

Beautifully.